I0591769

Where
Women Go

For a multi-racial company
of women and girls

by Tina Howe

|| SAMUEL FRENCH ||

FOR PRODUCTION INQUIRIES

UNITED STATES AND CANADA
info@concordtheatricals.com
1-866-979-0447

UNITED KINGDOM AND EUROPE
licensing@concordtheatricals.co.uk
020-7054-7298

Each title is subject to availability from Concord Theatricals Corp.,
depending upon country of performance. Please be aware that WHERE
WOMEN GO may not be licensed by Concord Theatricals Corp. in
your territory. Professional and amateur producers should contact the
nearest Concord Theatricals Corp. office or licensing partner to verify
availability.

No one shall make any changes in this title(s) for the purpose of production. No part of this book may be reproduced, stored in a retrieval system, scanned, uploaded, or transmitted in any form, by any means, now known or yet to be invented, including mechanical, electronic, digital, photocopying, recording, videotaping, or otherwise, without the prior written permission of the publisher. No one shall share this title(s), or any part of this title(s), through any social media or file hosting websites.

For all inquiries regarding motion picture, television, online/digital and other media rights, please contact Concord Theatricals Corp.

MUSIC AND THIRD-PARTY MATERIALS USE NOTE

Licensees are solely responsible for obtaining formal written permission from copyright owners to use copyrighted music and/or other copyrighted third-party materials (e.g. artworks, logos) in the performance of this play and are strongly cautioned to do so. If no such permission is obtained by the licensee, then the licensee must use only original music and materials that the licensee owns and controls. Licensees are solely responsible and liable for clearances of all third-party copyrighted materials, including without limitation music, and shall indemnify the copyright owners of the play(s) and their licensing agent, Concord Theatricals Corp., against any costs, expenses, losses and liabilities arising from the use of such copyrighted third-party materials by licensees. For music, please contact the appropriate music licensing authority in your territory for the rights to any incidental music.

IMPORTANT BILLING AND CREDIT REQUIREMENTS

If you have obtained performance rights to this title, please refer to your licensing agreement for important billing and credit requirements.

To the Dermatologist

CHARACTERS

in order of appearance

YU YAN – Receptionist, (Chinese, thirties to forties)

ISABELLA SANCHEZ – Receptionist, (Brazilian, thirties to forties)

HONEY GREEN – Receptionist, (Black, thirties to forties)

ACTING STUDENT – Exiting patients, (Any age and race)
(MRS. GOODYEAR, MEREDITH, J.T.)

ZILLA GOULD – Patient with burning spotted lower legs, (White, eighties)

MONIKA ISRAEL – Nurse, (Black, thirties)

DR. ANN PROCTER – Dermatologist, (Black, twenties)

MORRIS GOULD'S VOICE – Zilla's unseen husband, (White, eighties)

SETTING

The Upper West Side of New York City, spring, 2021. The stage is divided into three separate areas – the reception area of the Your Reflection Dermatology office which features a large mirror greeting incoming patients, an examining room with a reclining chair, and the Gould's living room suggested by two love seats.

Scene One

The Reception Area Of "Your Reflection" Dermatology

(AT RISE: We hear a lushly arranged American folk ballad from the 1960s.*)

*(**YU**, **ISABELLA** and **HONEY** dressed in white uniforms, wearing Covid masks are either on the phone or filling out medical forms. Several moments pass as we get used to the setting.)*

(An upset middle-aged patient on crutches heads for the exit.)

YU, ISABELLA & HONEY. Goodbye, Mrs. Goodyear. See you next week!

MRS. GOODYEAR (ACTING STUDENT). *(Disgusted.)* IN YOUR DREAMS!

(Several moments pass, then another bent-over female patient with a mask over her entire face rushes out the door, slamming the door behind her.)

---

* A license to produce *Where Women Go* does not include a performance license for any third-party or copyrighted music. Licensees should create an original composition or use music in the public domain. For further information, please see the Music and Third-Party Materials Use Note on page iii.

YU.	ISABELLA.	HONEY.
Bye, Meredith, takecare	See you tomorrow!	Looking good! Looking good!

MEREDITH (ACTING STUDENT). What did I do to deserve this?

(Moments later the doorbell rings.)

YU. *(In a sing-song voice.)* Come on in, Mrs. Gould the door's open.

(Nothing happens, then the bell rings again.)

(Louder.)

The door's open, just turn the knob to the right.

(We hear someone trying to turn the doorknob to the left.)

To the RIGHT, the RIGHT!

(A long silence then more struggling as the Simon and Garfunkel song fades.)

YU, ISABELLA & HONEY. *(Louder.)* TURN THE KNOB TO THE RIGHT SIDE, THE RIGHT SIDE!

(More frantic turning of the door knob, then knocking.)

ISABELLA. *(Rising to answer it.)* Hold on, hold on. I'll get it!

*(She opens the door and **ZILLA GOULD** tumbles in, knocking into her. She wears sandals, a plain white maxi skirt with a black T-shirt and carries a large cotton bag that says "WORDS MATTER".)*

ZILLA. Sorry, sorry, that's me and doctor's offices!

ZILLA.	ISABELLA.
Well, at least there's no broken glass or blood on the floor.	*(Straightening herself up.)* No problemo, welcome back, Mrs. Gould.

YU. Good old Zilla Gould with that infamous husband... WHO'S...*(Raising her hands to the others like a conductor.)*

YU, ISABELLA & HONEY. TOTALLY INVISIBLE!

YU. Who NONE of us have seen!

ISABELLA. EVER!

HONEY. Not even a fleeting view.

ZILLA. For me, it's been several YEARS!

YU. We don't even know if he really exists.

ZILLA. Join the club!

ISABELLA. Or is a pigment of *our* imagination.

THE OTHERS. "Figment" of your imagination...FIGMENT!

ISABELLA. Well, SOREE!

ZILLA. Not to worry he actually DOES exist, more or less... Mostly less.

YU, ISABELLA & HONEY. So, you say...

ZILLA. At least he used to. Good old...

YU.	ISABELLA.	HONEY.
Norris Gould!	Harris Gould!	Corliss Gould!

ZILLA. Morris Gould! MORRIS Gould!

(Brief pause.)

YU, ISABELLA & HONEY. GOOD OLD INVISIBLE MORRIS GOULD!

ZILLA. *(Conducting them.)* With the heart of...

ALL. GOLD!

ZILLA. *(Conducting them again.)* As well as being a...

ALL. FIRST RATE MUSICIAN!

ZILLA. On the...

ALL. ACCORDION!

> *(***ZILLA*** turns on her cell phone which has a recording of* **MORRIS** *playing the opening bars of a French ballad from the 1940s.* [*] *The receptionists clap and cheer as another patient zig-zags out of the office with half her face bandaged.)*

YU, ISABELLA & HONEY. *(Cheerfully to the departing patient.)* Bye, J.T., see you next month.

J.T. (ACTING STUDENT). *(Exiting.)* De tu boca al audífono de Dios. [*"From your mouth to God's hearing aid!"*]

> *(Slight pause.)*

ZILLA. *(Sitting down, looking around the office.)* Still no newspapers or magazines! I don't believe this!...A DERMATOLOGIST'S reception area with no high-end beauty magazines! Do you see us as some form of lower life with our rashes and peeling skin, who can't hold a candle to the more serious patients out there, suffering from brain cancer, collapsed lungs, or weak hearts?? I happen to have a disorder that would catapult me onto the evening news in a nanosecond! Film crews would be clamoring for the first shot of my blazing lower legs, believe me... Oh well, such is life

---

in a family-run dermatologist's office on the good old Upper West Side of New York City.

> (*Nothing happens for a good minute. Then* **MONIKA ISRAEL,** *the* **NURSE** *enters.*)

MONIKA. Well, hi there, Mrs. Gould, how are the legs?

ZILLA. Still attached, don't ask.

MONIKA. But of course, I'll ask, I'm your *nurse,* so follow me! Dr. Procter is ready to see you now.

> (**ZILLA** *limps out after her into Dr. Procter's examination room.*)

> (*Blackout.*)

Scene Two

The Examination Room Of "Your Reflection" Dermatology

DR. PROCTER. *(Dressed in an impressive doctor's outfit. Rises.)* Welcome, Mrs. Gould, welcome! *(Pointing to the examining chair.)* Have a seat, take a load off your feet.

ZILLA. *(Collapsing with a thud.)* FINALLY!

> (**MONIKA** *fusses with charts and bottles of lotion as...)*

DR. PROCTER. So, how are the legs treating you? Do they still tell you bedtime stories and sing arias from *Cosi Fan Tutti*?

ZILLA. Nice try, Dr. Procter, but you're not even close!

DR. PROCTER. I thought I'd seen everything when it comes to patients suffering from *Lichen planus*. But just to make sure you know what your condition is, I'd like you to join me, reciting what *"lichens"* actually ARE!

DR. PROCTER & ZILLA. *(Slow and deliberate in perfect unison.)* "Lichens are a complex life form that is a symbiotic partnership of two separate organisms, a fungus and an alga... The dominant partner is the fungus, which gives the lichen the majority of its characteristics from its thallus shape to its fruiting bodies... The alga can be either a green alga or a blue-green alga, otherwise known as cyanobacteria... Lichens are NOT in the plant family, but are a form of algae."

DR. PROCTER. *(Applauding.)* Very good, Zilla! EXCELLENT!...AND MOST IMPORTANT OF ALL, THAT FINAL SENTENCE ...

ZILLA. "Lichens are NOT in the plant family but are a form of ALGAE!"

DR. PROCTER. Very good, now tell us what algae IS.

ZILLA. "Algae is a single or multi-cellular organism that has no roots, stems, or leaves and is often found in water." Algae is NOT a plant.

DR. PROCTER. That's right. *(Eyeing* **MONIKA***.)* And once again...

DR. PROCTER, MONIKA & ZILLA. Algae is NOT a plant!

> *(A dramatic silence, then* **ZILLA** *starts to cry. She slowly lifts up her skirt. Small green dots are sprinkled over her lower legs.)*

DR. PROCTER & MONIKA. *(Bending down to examine them, then in unison.)* Something seems to be GROWING out of your legs!

ZILLA. But what? ALGAE IS NOT A PLANT!

DR. PROCTOR & MONIKA. *(In unison again.)* THEN WHAT IS THAT GROWING OUT OF HER LEGS?

> *(Dramatic pause.)*

DR. PROCTOR. *(In a little voice.)* Could we have a sniff?

ZILLA. Be my guest.

> *(***DR. PROCTOR** *and* **MONIKA** *lean over and sniff.)*

NOT TOO CLOSE! NOT TOO CLOSE, OR YOU'LL CATCH WHAT I'VE GOT!

> *(***DR. PROCTOR** *and* **MONIKA** *immediately leap back and try to get a whiff without getting too close. After several suspenseful moments...)*

DR. PROCTOR & MONIKA. It looks like tiny leaves... *(Bending closer to look.)* But from what plant?

DR. PROCTOR. Poison Ivy?

MONIKA. Ragweed?

DR. PROCTOR. Spinach?

MONIKA. Mistletoe?

DR. PROCTOR & MONIKA. HELP! HELLLLLLP!

YU, ISABELLA & HONEY. *(Rushing in to look.)* WHAT HAPPENED? WHAT HAPPENED?

DR. PROCTOR & MONIKA. YOU TELL US!

> *(They all gather around **ZILLA** as she breaks down sobbing.)*

> *(Blackout.)*

Scene Three

(Half an hour later. The Gould's simple living room with two matching love seats. We never see **MORRIS***, also in his eighties.)*

*(***ZILLA*** enters and plops down in one of the seats, undone.)*

ZILLA. *(In a loud, tearful voice to* **MORRIS**.*)* So how was my visit to the dermatologist, you ask? *(Long pause.)* Three guesses.

MORRIS' VOICE. *(Coming from off-stage.)* Hopeless, underwater, but kind.

ZILLA. How did you know?

MORRIS' VOICE. Because you keep getting worse.

ZILLA. *(Upset.)* I keep getting worse? How can you SAY that?

MORRIS' VOICE. Because it's true.

ZILLA. I keep getting WORSE?

MORRIS' VOICE. First it was a suspicious freckle here and there...

ZILLA. "Here and there..."

MORRIS' VOICE. Then a pre-cancerous mole there and here...

ZILLA. "There and here..."

MORRIS' VOICE. Then this "*Lichen planus*" that sounds like some sort of...rotten vegetable seeping out of your legs!

ZILLA. "ROTTEN *VEGETABLE* SEEPING OUT OF MY LEGS"? Thanks a lot!

(Pause.)

MORRIS' VOICE. OK...CAVIAR!

ZILLA. *(Hopeful.)* CAVIAR?

MORRIS' VOICE. BELUGA CAVIAR...the rarest, most delicious and expensive caviar harvested from the roe of the Beluga sturgeon...primarily found in the Caspian Sea bordered by Azerbaijan, Kazakhstan, and Russia, but also found in the...

ZILLA. QUICK, GET ME A SPOON!

MORRIS' VOICE. Come on, there's NO WAY we could afford Beluga caviar, not even one tiny egg with an eye dropper.

ZILLA. But here's the problem...whatever's growing down my legs feels sharp and spiny...more like the needles on the end of artichoke leaves.

MORRIS' VOICE. "THE NEEDLES ON THE END OF... ARTICHOKE LEAVES"?

ZILLA. Or blowfish prickers.

MORRIS' VOICE. "BLOWFISH PRICKERS"?

ZILLA. You heard me. BLOWFISH PRICKERS!

MORRIS' VOICE. I'M GETTING OUT OF HERE!

> *(We hear loud echoey footsteps running out of the room.)*

ZILLA. *(Sarcastic.)* Thanks a lot, Morris, thanks SO much for your ongoing love and support during these trying times! I don't know what I'd do without you!

> *(Blackout)*

Scene Four

The Examination Room Of "Your Reflection" Dermatology

(It's three days later, a very nervous **MONIKA ISRAEL** *has just led* **ZILLA** *into the Examination Room. She limps toward the examination chair and sinks into it with a thud as* **MONIKA** *adjusts her chair.)*

MONIKA. Welcome back, Zilla, welcome! We've all been taking bets about what sorts of weeds or maybe even *spices* might be popping out of your legs.

DR. PROCTOR. Now, now Monika, you weren't hired to frighten our patients.

MONIKA. But who knows, it could be just salt and pepper.

ZILLA. *(Sneaking a look at her legs, horrified.)* "Salt and pepper"?

MONIKA. You're by far our most interesting patient! I wouldn't be surprised if we found traces of cinnamon between your toes.

DR. PROCTOR. *(Outraged.)* Monika, PLEASE!

MONIKA. Or vanilla seeping out of your...

DR. PROCTOR. THAT'S ENOUGH!

MONIKA. Toenails.

ZILLA. But *Lichen planus* isn't a plant, it's an ALGAE!

(Dead silence for a bit too long.)

Don't ask me what's going on, because Morris is no help. No help AT ALL!

MONIKA. *(Softly.)* Three cheers for Morris Gould!

DR. PROCTOR. *(In a threatening voice.)* Monika??

MONIKA.	**ZILLA.**
Sorry, sorry...I'll behave.	It's not just weird, it's *painful!*

DR. PROCTOR. *(Grabbing a magnifying glass.)* Let me have a good look at those legs! *(She does, then amazed.)* Oh My God! MY GOD! OUR MOST HOLY GOD!

ZILLA. What? WHAT...? WHAT IS IT?

DR. PROCTOR. *(Pulling small specimens out of her legs, smelling them carefully, one by one.)* PARSLEY... SAGE...ROSEMARY and...

ZILLA & MONIKA. NO WAY!

DR. PROCTOR. THYME!

ZILLA. But *Lichen planus* isn't a plant, it's an ALGAE!

DR. PROCTOR. Then Zilla, please remind Monika what an algae IS!

ZILLA. *(Raising her voice.)* A simple, nonflowering, and typically AQUATIC PLANT of a large group that includes the seaweeds and many single-celled forms. Algae contain chlorophyll but...LACK TRUE STEMS, ROOTS, LEAVES AND VASCULAR TISSUE.

> *(Slight pause, then* **DR. PROCTOR** *and* **MONIKA** *sing the ballad that plays in the background to start the play.*)*
>
> *(As they sing,* **YU, ISABELLA** *and* **HONEY** *enters and join them with rising gusto.)*

---

* A license to produce *Where Women Go* does not include a performance license for any third-party or copyrighted music. Licensees should create an original composition or use music in the public domain. For further information, please see the Music and Third-Party Materials Use Note on page iii.

(The lights are abruptly turned off and the room is plunged into darkness for a few seconds, then suddenly a spot light shines on **ZILLA** *who emerges reborn.)*

ZILLA. Thank you...Thank you very much...now we can proceed. I'm naturally shocked at what's been going on in my body, more than shocked, since it almost feels like some sort of divine intervention...as if I've suddenly shed my identity, becoming part of another species, yet keeping my voice and the ability to express myself. A human female spice rack, if you will.

(The others whistle and applaud from the floor.)

(Making up a song and singing it.[*])

I HAVE DERMATOLOGICAL MAGIC UP MY SLEEVE WITH PARA-PSYCHOLOGICAL GIFTS YOU CAN NOT BELIEVE!

ALL EXCEPT ZILLA. *(The others applaud in unison.)* Nice, nice...very nice...

ZILLA. *(Continuing her song.)*

MY LEGS SIZZLE AND BURN, TURNING BRIGHT RED, GROWING RARE SPICES THAT...

(She pauses.)

ALL EXCEPT DR. PROCTOR & ZILLA. *(Finishing for her.)* "Unscrew your head!"

(The others applaud, then.)

ALL EXCEPT ZILLA. More, more!

ZILLA.

BUT OH, THE FRAGRANCE THAT THEY SET LOOSE...

---

[*] A license to produce *Where Women Go* does not include a performance license for any third-party or copyrighted music. Licensees should create an original composition or use music in the public domain. For further information, please see the Music and Third-Party Materials Use Note on page iii.

ALL EXCEPT DR. PROCTOR & ZILLA.
> HARK, WHO'S COMING? IS THAT MOTHER GOOSE?

ZILLA.
> BAA BAA BLACK SHEEP HAVE YOU ANY WOOL? YES SIR, YES SIR, ONE TRUNK FULL!

> > *(All except* **DR. PROCTOR** *burst into wild cheers and applause.)*

DR. PROCTOR. *(Trying to control herself.)* OK, OK, that's enough...

ALL EXCEPT DR. PROCTOR & ZILLA.
> BECAUSE WE'RE MORE PRECIOUS THAN DIAMONDS IN THE...

ALL EXCEPT DR. PROCTOR. ROUGH!

ZILLA. Here's the thing, these erupting spices are very painful because of their strength. I don't know the biological word for it, but parsley, sage, rosemary and thyme each have their own...ZEST! As a result, they have the power to spread their unique taste over an entire serving of rice, spaghetti, or linguine. Since they all grow in the same soil, they can't help sharing their potency... Oh my God, did you hear what I just said? Since they grow in the same SOIL...MY LEGS ARE NOW FILLED WITH DIRT! Soon earth worms and caterpillars will be crawling up and down my back and between my breasts...

DR. PROCTOR. GIRLS, GIRLS, THAT'S ENOUGH!

ZILLA. *(Cheerful.)* On the other hand...

YU, ISABELLA & HONEY. *(Expectantly "On the other hand"?)*

> *(Long pause.)*

"ON THE OTHER HAND..."?

ZILLA.   There's something...What's the right word? "Powerful!" "Extraordinary...!" *"NEWSWORTHY..."* About spices growing in my lower legs! I sound like some ancient Greek goddess who fed the hungry with fruits from her own body.

YU, ISABELLA, & HONEY.   Nice...nice.

DR. PROCTER.   It would certainly bring new patients into the office!

MONIKA.   They'd come in droves just to *watch!*

YU, ISABELLA & HONEY.   Then we'd *sell* her spices in small glass bottles shaped like her legs.

ZILLA.   But it's the variety of spices, of spices that grow in my lower legs, their colors, size, flavors, and tastes... It's the range of their variety that's so mind-blowing...

THE OTHERS.   "Range of their variety."

ZILLA.   Just name a spice and I'll toot this whistle to let you know if I have it. *(She blows up and down on a harmonica, then hits one note.)*

YU.   Allspice!

> *(Another toot.)*

ISABELLA.   Anise!

> *(Toot.)*

HONEY.   Basil!

> *(Toot.)*

MONIKA.   Bay leaves!

> *(Toot.)*

DR. PROCTOR.   Caraway!

> *(Toot.)*

YU. Chili powder!

　　　(Toot.)

ISABELLA. Cilantro!

　　　(Toot.)

MONIKA. Cinnamon!

　　　(Toot.)

DR. PROCTER. Cloves!

　　　(Her toots go faster and faster.)

YU. Dill weed!

　　　(Toot.)

ISABELLA. Fennel!

　　　(Toot.)

HONEY. Garlic!

　　　(Toot.)

MONIKA. Ginger!

　　　(Toot.)

DR. PROCTER. Mustard!

　　　(Toot.)

YU. Nutmeg!

　　　(Toot.)

ISABELLA. Oregano!

　　　(Toot.)

HONEY. Paprika!

(Toot.)

MONIKA. *(Singing it.*)*
PARSLEY ...

(Toot.)

DR. PROCTER. *(Singing it.)*
SAGE ...

(Toot.)

YU. *(Singing it.)*
ROSEMARY ...

(Toot.)

ISABELLA. *(Singing it.)*
AND THYME.

(Lots of toots, then a brief silence, before **HONEY** *ends with a flourish.)*

HONEY. Pepper, salt, sugar, tarragon, and vanilla!

(Wild applause and cheering, then silence.)

ZILLA. *(Softly.)* What did I tell you?

DR. PROCTER. Zilla, Zilla, you're one in a million...

MONIKA. Billion!

YU, ISABELLA & HONEY. TRILLION AND GODZILLION!

(Pause.)

---

* A license to produce *Where Women Go* does not include a performance license for any third-party or copyrighted music. Licensees should create an original composition or use music in the public domain. For further information, please see the Music and Third-Party Materials Use Note on page iii.

MORRIS' VOICE. Now the challenge is figuring out how to USE this precious gift for the benefit of mankind.

ALL EXCEPT ZILLA. How the hell did *he* get in here?

ZILLA. That's Morris for you... He has the ability to show up in my life whenever he wants, but I'm denied access to return the favor.

MORRIS' VOICE. There, there, Zilla, don't get all upset on me now, you were doing really great! I loved how you were all able to tick off the variety of spices that pop out of your legs alphabetically, I mean, that took real imagination on everyone's part!

ZILLA. But then YOU butted in, like you always do!

MORRIS' VOICE. Sorry, sorry...

> (**ZILLA** *bares her teeth and growls at him.*)

I'll behave.

ZILLA. Better than that, you'll LEAVE...so GOODBYE! Have a nice trip.

> (*She snaps her fingers, we hear his body zipping through space.*)

MORRIS' VOICE. (*From a distance.*) Goodbye.

> (*An awkward silence.*)

ZILLA. You have no idea how painful it is when spices break through your skin. My next fear is obviously what if something *bigger* starts crashing through.

MONIKA. Something *bigger?*

YU. (*Excited.*) Brownies!

ISABELLE. Donuts!

HONEY. Lady Fingers!

ZILLA. But they don't grow in the soil.

YU. Strawberries!

ISABELLE. Oranges!

HONEY. WATERMELONS!

> (**ZILLA** *runs out in tears.*)

DR. PROCTER. Girls, girls, behave yourselves!

> (*Blackout.*)

Scene Five

(It's one year later, the waiting room of the office has been turned into the very successful "Zilla's Spicy Café." Numerous packed tables and chairs now fill the room. ZILLA sits at one of them. YU, ISABELLE and HONEY are now dressed as waitresses with "Zilla's Spicy Café" written on their aprons and caps as they glide from table to table, carrying trays laden with pastries and fine European desserts.)

YU. *(Stopping at a table.)* What's your pleasure today? Our Maltese Brandy Muffins or delicate French Lady Fingers?

ISABELLE. *(At another table.)* Can we interest you in tortillas frosted with Anise-Infused Sherbet?

HONEY. How about some Key Lime Pie served with Hearts of Palm and a healthy shot of Drambuie?

ZILLA. *(At another table.)* Just hearing you reel off all the offerings tonight makes my heart race.

YU, ISABELLE & HONEY. *(Under their breath.)* And hopefully your lower legs as well! WOOO! WOOO! WOOO! WOOO!

ZILLA. WAAA! WEEE! WOOO! WUUUU!

DR. PROCTER & MONIKA. *(Entering and speaking simultaneously.)* Did we just hear a familiar cheer?

ZILLA. *(Louder.)* OH MY GOD, HERE I GO AGAIN! STAND BACK FOR THE MIRACLE OF THE DECADE...! THE SPICES FROM MY LEGS NOW COME BOTTLED AND READY TO DISTRIBUTE... WHOOEEEE! *(She reaches under the table and starts hauling up the latest harvest as the lights slowly fade.)*

To Subway

CHARACTERS

in order of appearance

PUDDING – Server, (Latinx, thirties)
SAL – Server, (African, thirties)
HANNAH – Dedicated customer, (American, fifties)
CLARA – Her reluctant friend, (American, fifties)
ALIDA VALLI – Actress from the movie, *The Third Man*, (Czech, forties)

SETTING

The interior of a Subway sandwich store. A long glass counter is center stage, filled with a variety of meats running into a selection of salad choices. Assorted seating areas are available on either side. Two female servers are posted at opposite ends of the counter, but since there aren't any customers, they're frozen in place.

*(AT RISE: The lights rise on two female servers from a Subway shop in NYC. They're gazing at the door hoping to see someone enter. No one does. **SAL** sighs, then **PUDDING**. They wait two minutes more, nothing. **PUDDING** straightens her cap. **SAL** straightens her uniform. **PUDDING** makes an angry face. **SAL** joins her. **PUDDING** emits a loud sigh. **SAL** an even louder one. **PUDDING** pretends to cry, shaking her shoulders with sobs. **SAL** joins her. They get carried away and soon are striking all kinds of impatient poses. **HANNAH** and **CLARA**, two women in their fifties finally enter.)*

PUDDING & SAL. HOORAY, HOORAY, HANNAH'S FINALLY HERE! Hannah's here!

HANNAH. *(To **CLARA**.)* Easy, easy...I brought my old friend Clara who's come to visit me. This is the first time she's ever been to a Subway in her entire *life!*

PUDDING & SAL. No way!

CLARA. *(Depressed.)* What could I do? She INSISTED!

HANNAH. *(Enthusiastically.)* Her very FIRST time, no less!

CLARA. She had to drag me!

HANNAH. Just wait, Clara, I'll bet you a million dollars, you've never had such TASTY food in your ENTIRE life!

CLARA. Dream on!

HANNAH. *(Pulling one out of her pocket.)* How about a dime, then?

CLARA. No way, <u>HAM!</u>

PUDDING & SAL. *Ham?*

HANNAH.	**CLARA.**
She's always called me "Ham."	I've always called her "Ham."

PUDDING & SAL. *"Ham" with an "M"?*

CLARA. What's wrong? You have a problem with "Ham"?

PUDDING.	**SAL.**
But shouldn't it be "Han"?	Not "Ham," but "Han"!

HANNAH.	**CLARA.**
No "Ham"!	I said, it's always been "Ham"!

PUDDING.	**SAL.**
Well, sorree!	But how could have *we* have known that

CLARA. Well, pardon me for living.

PUDDING.	**SAL.**
Hannah. Take it easy, girl!	Well, sorree!
Calm down, Clar!	

    (A tense silence.)

HANNAH. *(Approaching the counter.)* Get a load of all this luscious food beckoning us from the counter... I mean, when have you ever seen such a comprehensive spread? Huh? HUH? Check out the variety of *meats*: Turkey, Black Forest Ham, Spicy Italian, Sweet Onion Chicken Teriyaki, Meatballs Marina, Cold Cut Combo, Rotisserie Style Chicken, Roast Beef, Buffalo Chicken, and Veggie Delight...I mean, *come on!*

(A longer tense silence.)

What will it be? The Sweet Onion Chicken Teriyaki Meatballs Marinara, or Veggie Delight?

CLARA. Veggie *Delight?* What's "delightful" about veggies?

PUDDING. *(In rapid fire.)* Their freshness!

SAL. Cut!

PUDDING. Size!

SAL. Price!

PUDDING. And *originality!*

CLARA. How can a vegetable be "original"?

SAL & PUDDING. By being served at SUBWAY!

HANNAH. Which only serves the BEST!

SAL & PUDDING. The BEST of the Best!

SAL, PUDDING & HANNAH. AND THEN SOME! *(Breaking into cheers.)*

CLARA. *(Hands over her ears.)* OK...OK...

> *(**SAL**, **PUDDING** and **HANNAH** keep cheering.)*

(Yelling into an imaginary bullhorn, very loud.) THAT'S ENOUGH!

> *(Dead silence.)*

SAL & PUDDING. *(In a whisper.)* Where did she get that imaginary bull horn?

HANNAH. I forgot to warn you, Clara's an extraordinary woman who specializes in sudden surprises. *(Lowering her voice.)* Once I saw her turn herself into a spoonful of Jello.

SAL & PUDDING. No...

HANNAH. And another time, an oar in a hummingbird cage...

SAL & PUDDING. "An oar in a *hummingbird* cage"?

HANNAH & CLARA. God's truth!

SAL.	PUDDING.
Why a *hummingbird* cage?	How would it *fit?*

HANNAH. Who knows!

PUDDING. But hummingbirds don't travel in boats!

CLARA. You've never seen a *hummingbird* rowing a boat?

PUDDING. NO! Have YOU?

HANNAH. Many times! *(Pause.)* Come on, can't you take a joke?

> (**PUDDING** *and* **SAL** *moan in frustration, then silence.)*

SAL. OK, ladies, what'll it be?

CLARA. *(Reading the chart again.)* Let's see, Turkey, Black Forest Ham, Spicy Italian...

HANNAH. We should each get something different so we can share.

CLARA. But what if I don't like what you ordered?

HANNAH. Tough titty.

PUDDING. *(Bursting into laughter.)* "Tough titty"?? I haven't heard *that* in ages!

SAL. That's because tough titties don't frequent Subways!

PUDDING. Just perky ones!

SAL. You mean, *discerning* ones!

CLARA. *(To* **HANNAH.***)* Wow...classy adjective!

HANNAH. Of course she said, "discerning," she's a server at Subway! What did you expect?

SAL. Why thank you!

HANNAH. My pleasure.

CLARA. I think I'm starting to figure out why you like "Subways" so much – their choice of dishes and the enthusiasm of the servers!

PUDDING. Plus, intelligence! *Intelligence!* Both Sal and I aced the college boards.

HANNAH. True!

CLARA. I'm impressed.

HANNAH. One went to Harvard and the other Yale!

CLARA. Noooo!

PUDDING, SAL & HANNAH. God's truth!

HANNAH. At the same time! I should know because I visited them when they were undergraduates!

CLARA. So, let's hear you sing your college songs.

PUDDING & SAL. We're *servers*, we don't sing while we work.

CLARA. Well, pardon me for living!

HANNAH. Come on Clar, take it easy.

CLARA. Take it easy in a *Subway?* But then I'll get pickpocketed by a starving customer!

PUDDING & SAL. Thank you for your high opinion of us!

HANNAH. OK, OK, ENOUGH WITH THE DICKERING!

(Dead silence.)

(**ALIDA VALLI** *enters playing the gypsy jazz theme song from a 1940s mystery movie on a zither.**)

PUDDING & SAL. *What the hell??*

PUDDING, SAL, HANNAH & CLARA. LOUDER! LOUDER!

(**ALIDA** *turns up the volume.*)

(*Cheering, applauding and dancing.*) I LOVE IT, LOVE IT, LOVE IT!

Why on earth...? How on earth...? I don't understand... What's happening...?

(*Silence.*)

ALIDA. (*Approaching* **CLARA**, *in a friendly voice.*) Hannah invited you here to give you a treat because she was eager to share something very special with you...YES?

(*Long pause.*)

CLARA. (*Shyly.*) Really?

THE OTHERS. (*In sympathy.*) Awwwww...

ALIDA. So why won't you join her?

(**CLARA** *doesn't move.*)

(*Leaning closer to* **CLARA**, *softly.*) Come on, *join* her. Do it for me...*and the third man!*

(*A pause.*)

CLARA. Will you keep playing?

---

* A license to produce *Where Women Go* does not include a performance license for any third-party or copyrighted music. Licensees should create an original composition or use music in the public domain. For further information, please see the Music and Third-Party Materials Use Note on page iii.

ALIDA. YOU BET! *(She resumes.)*

CLARA. OK, OK! *(Pause, then to* **PUDDING** *and* **SAL**.*)* MAKE IT A COMBO OF BLACK FOREST EEL, ROTISSERIE STYLE CANARY AND RAW EAGLE LEGS, WITH A SPRINKLING OF MULE EARS ON THE SIDE!

PUDDING & SAL. You got it: A combo of Black Forest Eel, Rotisserie-Style Canary, and Raw Eagle Legs with a sprinkling of Mule Ears on the side, coming up!!

CLARA. *(Faster and faster.)* Grasshopper faces...

ALIDA. Frog tails...

CLARA. Turkey hearts...

ALIDA. Beef hooves...

CLARA. Sheep ears...

PUDDING. Ox lips! You won't know what hit you, it's such a thrilling fusion of tastes.

SAL. A once-in-a-lifetime orgy that can only be served at Subway, *so dig in and ENJOY!*

CLARA. *(Digging it.)* WOW, SENSATIONAL! GORGING ABOVE AND BELOW GOOD OLD VIENNA!!

The End

Shopping

CHARACTERS

in order of appearance

ED SINGH – Owner of the stand, (Egyptian, fifties to sixties)

KITTY BUCKLE – Playwright, (White, eighties)

SANDY WRENCH – Cellist, (American, thirties to forties)

BLOSSOM PICK – Plays the recorder, (American, thirties to forties)

FREDDIE GONZALES – Plays the guitar, (South American woman, thirties to forties)

NAMELESS UNKEMPT MYSTERY WOMAN – (Any age from anywhere)

SOPRANO WOMAN WITH A BEAUTIFUL VOICE – (Any age from anywhere)

PENNY HO – High school student, (Teenager)

CALLIOPE SNOW – High school student, (American, Teenager)

SILENT MAN WEARING A PARACHUTE – Keeps taking the cover ups off their hangers, lowering his mask to smell them. (Any age from anywhere)

SETTING

Ed Singh's one-man outdoor shopping stand in front of a popular grocery store on the Upper West Side of New York City. It's the beginning of October 2022, at the height of the Covid epidemic. Colorful Indian cover-ups flutter on collapsible racks on either side of his table, along with more familiar accessories made in the US – scarves, gloves, socks and woolen caps. His customers are almost exclusively women. Everyone including Ed, wears a mask.

(AT RISE: Haunting Egyptian music plays as the lights rise on **ED** *who's finishing setting up his stand for the day, fussing over his cover ups, making sure they're hanging neatly.* Two women finally appear, but they walk right past him, then four more, then finally all the cast members, dressed in a wild variety of outfits who don't bother to stop. Poor* **ED** *becomes increasingly agitated, making increasingly dramatic gestures around his goods.* **KITTY BUCKLE** *finally stops, intrigued by two very different pairs of gloves. First, she tries one from a plain green pair, then one from a wildly patterned pair and then back to the green one – back and forth multiple times.)*

KITTY. I can't decide between them!

ED. So, I see!

KITTY. They work so well together! *(Putting on a show of each glove getting to know the other.)*

ED. Clever, clever...very clever.

KITTY. They have an uncanny way of completing each other. *(Lifting up one hand.)* The plain one delighting in the wildly patterned garden of delights...

ED. Interesting, interesting.

---

* A license to produce *Where Women Go* does not include a performance license for any third-party or copyrighted music. Licensees should create an original composition or use music in the public domain. For further information, please see the Music and Third-Party Materials Use Note on page iii.

KITTY. *(Raising the other.)* Which in turn, is grateful to be noticed by such a colorful one.

ED. You've got quite an eye there! Just like me, except I'm Egyptian and you're clearly American, but still, you should buy both pairs since they've probably been waiting their whole lives for the other to show up. *(Quickly picking them up.)* I'll wrap up each pair for you.

KITTY. *(Stopping him.)* No, no, I can only buy one.

ED. But they've finally *found* each other!

KITTY. What can I say? Life isn't fair.

ED. You can say *that* again.

　　　　(Pause.)

KITTY. *(Near tears.) What can I say? Life isn't fair!*

ED. At least they shared this moment of intimacy together.

　　　　*(**KITTY** breaks down sobbing then silence.)*

So, I'm guessing you're hoping I'll give you both pairs for the price of one!

KITTY. Not at all, you probably have twelve starving Egyptian children at home.

ED. *(Upset.)* Thanks so much for the insulting image, it's been a pleasure talking with you, what else can I show you? How about some fingers chopped off from the mummy we worship in the basement.

KITTY. *(Nears tears again.)* I'm sorry, I don't know what's wrong with me today.

ED. *(Offering her his hand.)* Not to worry, it's living through all these Covid pandemics.

KITTY. *(Taking it.)* Please forgive me.

ED. See how our two hands fit together? Mine, Egyptian, and yours, American? What state are you from?

KITTY. *(Playfully.)* Guess!

> *(**ED** and **KITTY** recite lyrics from a musical referencing a state in Egypt.*)*

> *(A lovely pause.)*

ED & KITTY. *(Applauding.)* You knew it, you knew it!

ED. So come on, buy the second pair as well.

KITTY. BUT IT DOESN'T MAKE SENSE TO BUY TWO PAIRS OF GLOVES WHEN I ONLY NEED ONE!

> *(A tense silence.)*

ED.	**KITTY**.
You're right, you're right.	This is an artistic conundrum I've got to figure out.

> *(More silence.)*

| Who knew buying a pair of could be so complicated? | Life has a way of keeping gloves you on your toes! |

ED. It's because you're a sensitive observer who senses the kinship between them.

KITTY. Flattery will get you nowhere. *(Waving one of them in front of him.)* It's just that this one seems to be asking its opposite an important question.

ED. You're right.

---

* A license to produce *Where Women Go* does not include a performance license for any third-party or copyrighted music. Licensees should create an original composition or use music in the public domain. For further information, please see the Music and Third-Party Materials Use Note on page iii.

KITTY. See? You're just as intrigued as they are!

ED. I was just wondering what the solution is, since I didn't know gloves had opinions, let alone the ability to express them.

KITTY. OF COURSE, GLOVES HAVE OPINIONS, HAVEN'T YOU EVER SEEN BOXING GLOVES IN THE RING? *(She whispers to the gloves to start boxing. They do.)* TAKE THAT YOU IDIOT...*(The other returns the hit.)* OH NO YOU DON'T, YOU CRETIN... PREPARE TO DIE!

> *(And soon the gloves are at war with each other. At that moment,* **SANDY WRENCH,** **BLOSSOM PICK** *and* **FREDDIE GONZALES,** *carrying their hidden instruments, stop at the table, mesmerized by Kitty's show. Having an audience makes her even more dramatic.)*

(As one glove.) TAKE THAT AND THAT, YOU MORON! *(And then the other.)* OH NO YOU DON'T, YOU ASSHOLE, PREPARE TO DIE! *(To the women.)* I seem to have fallen into a dilemma here: each pair of gloves was initially fascinated by the other, but now they're suddenly sworn enemies. What happened?

> *(She stages an even more dramatic fight between them, ripping off fingers.)*

ED. *(Like a barker.)* "STEP RIGHT UP AND SEE THE ONCE-IN-A LIFETIME-FIGHT BETWEEN THE HANDSOMELY TAILORED GREEN GLOVE AND THE MULTI-PATTERNED WILD ONE, *BOTH* NOW MISSING FINGERS!"

BLOSSOM. *(Taking her recorder out of its case.)* Easy, easy, you poor things, there's no reason to be fighting like this. I can tell at a glance that each of you is blessed with different attributes. The green glove is cleverly designed, hiding its inherent beauty in subtle ways, whereas the technicolor one is urging you to add more color and joy to your life.

(She raises her recorder to her lips and plays a beautiful recording of "Greensleeves.")

ED. *(In raptures.)* "Greensleeves"! No way... I don't believe this!

KITTY. Where am I?

> *(**SANDY** pulls her cello out of its case, sits down and plays the song, joining **BLOSSOM** with the melody.)*

I've died and gone to heaven.

ED. And I'm right next to you on an adjacent cloud!

> *(**FREDDIE** now pulls her guitar out of its case and accompanies them with an enchanting trio.)*

Where are the newspaper reporters and photographers when you need them?

KITTY. I don't know what to say.

ED. You don't have to say anything, we're doing just fine!

> *(The musicians keep playing their accompaniments as **KITTY** brings her two gloves closer and closer together until they're whispering to each other as if each one has a great secret, but they soon realize they're sharing the same secret, so they hug and separate, politely bowing to each other.)*

KITTY. BRAVO! BRAVO! Well done!

SANDY. *(To **ED.**)* "BRILLIANTLY done!" would be better!

---

* A license to produce *Where Women Go* does not include a performance license for any third-party or copyrighted music. Licensees should create an original composition or use music in the public domain. For further information, please see the Music and Third-Party Materials Use Note on page iii.

BLOSSOM. MORE! MORE!

FREDDIE. How about "PLAY IT AGAIN"!?

ED. That was sensational...! Fantabulous...! Once in a lifetime!

KITTY & THE THREE MUSICIANS. HERE! HERE!

    (Silence.)

ED. *(With high energy.)* So how about a little SHOPPING now! Looking over my unique and well-made winter wares from all over the world... Genuine fur earmuffs, hand woven socks and mittens, and artfully designed coverings for ears, feet and hands. Come on ladies, let's see a little competition and energy here. I'll give you 'til the count of five to scan the merchandise, and then the first one to snatch her favorite item, gets to buy it!

    One...TWO...THREE...FOUR...FIVE!

> *(The women dive into the goods, grabbing what they want, often trying to snatch something that's already been taken. Soon they're fighting each other, screaming at the same time, getting into bizarre positions of offense and defense.)*

KITTY. *(Repeated dialogue.)* HEY, I SAW THAT FIRST, WHAT THE HELL DO YOU THINK YOU'RE DOING?

SANDY. *(Repeated dialogue:)* OH NO YOU DON'T! THAT'S MINE! I SAID, THAT'S MINE!

BLOSSOM. *(Sings:)*
    OLD MACDONALD HAD A FARM,
    E, I, E, I, O...
    AND ON THAT FARM HE HAD A PIG,
    E, I, E, I, O...
    WITH A SNORT-SNORT HERE,

AND A SNORT-SNORT THERE, *(Doing it.)*
E, I, E, I, O...
OLD MACDONALD HAD A FARM
AND ON THAT FARM, HE HAD A HORSE,
E, I, E, I, O...
WITH A WHINNY HERE,
AND A WHINNY THERE, *(Doing it.)*
E, I, E, I, O...
OLD MACDONALD HAD A FARM
AND ON THAT FARM HE HAD A COW...*(She moos.)*
...HAD A SHEEP...*(She baas.)*
HAD A HEN...*(She clucks...and starts over again with the pig.)*

FREDDIE. *(Adlibs: swears in Spanish, starting softly but getting louder and louder as she goes.)*

ED. Ladies, ladies, please... Take it easy... What's going on? Come on, act your age! You're destroying my entire inventory. I've been running this stand for over two decades and have never seen behavior like this! And from *women,* who are supposed to be the gentler sex... I don't understand!

> **(ED** *suddenly blows a whistle very loud. Silence as the women return what they grabbed, neaten the piles of goods, link arms, bow their heads in shame, curtsy and exit. A slower version of "Greensleeves" plays.*)*

Good God, what's happening? Where am I? WHO am I? Peace has suddenly descended, I'm still alive and my goods look more tempting than ever! Those women were goddesses who came to anoint my merchandise, making it glow!

---

* A license to produce *Where Women Go* does not include a performance license for any third-party or copyrighted music. Licensees should create an original composition or use music in the public domain. For further information, please see the Music and Third-Party Materials Use Note on page iii.

(His stand starts to glow as **NAMELESS**, *an* **UNKEMPT MYSTERY WOMAN**, *stops at the stand, puts on a pair of earmuffs and looks at herself in the mirror.)*

ED. Nice, nice...very becoming!

(She quickly takes them off, and puts on another pair.)

Good choice!

(Then takes those off for another.)

You're so attractive, it's hard to choose.

(Going faster and faster, she takes off three more pairs roughly throwing them all over the stand when she's done.)

NOW SEE HERE, THIS IS A SERIOUS OUTDOOR BUSINESS! I WILL NOT HAVE CUSTOMERS TAKE ADVANTAGE OF ME, DESTROYING MY MERCHANDISE, UNDERSTOOD? *(He then repeats this even louder in Egyptian Arabic.)*

*(**NAMELESS** picks up each hat she tried on, wipes it off, neatly puts it back where she found it and then exits.)*

(Yelling after her "many thanks" in Egyptian Arabic.) *Moutashaker Awi*. Well, that was fast – to say nothing about being amazing. IF YOU'RE FREE THIS EVENING, WHY NOT STOP BY FOR A LITTLE NIGHT CAP!

(He turns on an invisible switch that plays a Strauss waltz and starts dancing around his stand.*)

It's such a pity my shoppers aren't aware of how cultured we Egyptians are, having been around for eons before these deaf, blind and mute Westerners sailed over from the Skittish Isles!

*(**PENNY HO** and **CALLIOPE SNOW**, two high school students from the area show up, see **ED** dancing and quickly join him, singing, "LA, LA, LA, LA, LA, LA, LA" in time with the music. He joins them and they start dancing in strange patterns, then **ED** stops.)*

FINALLY...! A PAIR OF SHOPPERS WITH A LITTLE BRIO! What treasures in my store have caught your attention?

*(**PENNY** and **CALLIOPE** immediately start trying on as many items as they can – cover ups, hats, gloves and earmuffs as **ED** tries to stop them.)*

EASY...EASY...WHAT DO YOU THINK YOU'RE DOING? I SIMPLY ASKED YOU WHAT MIGHT HAVE CAUGHT YOUR INTEREST! I DIDN'T TELL YOU TO START TRYING THINGS ON!

(But then they suddenly start dressing him, dragging him in front of the mirror, placing furry earmuffs on his head and gloves on his hands.)

PENNY. See how handsome you look in your wares?

---

* A license to produce *Where Women Go* does not include a performance license for any third-party or copyrighted music. Licensees should create an original composition or use music in the public domain. For further information, please see the Music and Third-Party Materials Use Note on page iii.

CALLIOPE. You could catch any woman in the neighborhood!

PENNY. Or *man*, for that matter – your choice!

> (**PENNY** *and* **CALLIOPE** *start singing a romantic, golden-age musical classic, reaching out to* **ED** *who joins them, round and round the booth.** *They sing and dance with rising energy as* **A SILENT MAN WEARING A PARACHUTE** *starts taking the cover ups off their hangers and smelling them.* **PENNY** *and* **CALLIOPE** *spot him much sooner than* **ED** *and keep nudging each other, laughing, until* **ED** *finally sees the guy too, rushing up to him.*)

ED. HOLY SAINT JEHOSOPHAT, WHAT THE HELL DO YOU THINK YOU'RE DOING? *(Louder.)* HELP, MURDER, POLICE, A MANIAC IN A PARACHUTE JUST FLEW INTO MY STAND AND IS SMELLING MY MERCHANDISE!

> (*Dead silence as everyone freezes.* **THE SILENT MAN WEARING A PARACHUTE** *gives* **ED** *the finger, then takes another cover up, smells it, inhales even deeper, then lifts up his hand, making an OK gesture.*)

PENNY & CALLIOPE. He likes it! HE LIKES IT!

ED. *(For a moment he's pleased.).* He likes it! *(Then noting that he's smelling it more dramatically, gets angry again.)* But customers are NOT allowed to fly into the merchandise and SMELL it! Give a local merchant a break!

---

* A license to produce *Where Women Go* does not include a performance license for any third-party or copyrighted music. Licensees should create an original composition or use music in the public domain. For further information, please see the Music and Third-Party Materials Use Note on page iii.

(*THE SILENT MAN WEARING A PARACHUTE* *then leans over towards* **PENNY** *and smells her jacket, grinning from ear to ear.*)

PENNY. I smell good, I smell good!

(**CALLIOPE** *approaches him. He smells her jacket and feigns violently throwing up.*)

CALLIOPE. *(Trying to hit him.)* THANKS A LOT, ASSHOLE, WELL DONE! YOU REALLY KNOW YOUR WAY AROUND WOMEN!

(*THE SILENT MAN WEARING A PARACHUTE* *starts running away as his parachute billows out after him.*)

(Chasing him.) Oh no, you don't, you flying maniac! I'M RIGHT ON YOUR RISING HEELS!

PENNY. *(Running after her.)* Wait for me! Wait for me!

(*And once again* **ED** *is alone at his stand. He walks back and forth examining his wares, making sure everything is in the right place. He starts singing "The Star Spangled Banner" in a dramatic voice.**)

ED.

O SAY CAN YOU SEE, BY THE DAWN'S EARLY LIGHT,
WHAT SO PROUDLY WE HAILED AT THE TWILIGHT'S LAST
    GLEAMING.
WHOSE BROAD STRIPES AND BRIGHT STARS THROUGH
    THE PERILOUS FIGHT
O'ER THE RAMPARTS WE WATCHED WERE SO GALLANTLY
    STREAMING?
AND THE ROCKET'S RED GLARE, THE BOMBS BURSTING IN
    AIR,

---

* A license to produce *Where Women Go* does not include a performance license for any third-party or copyrighted music. Licensees should create an original composition or use music in the public domain. For further information, please see the Music and Third-Party Materials Use Note on page iii.

GAVE PROOF THROUGH THE NIGHT THAT OUR FLAG WAS
STILL THERE,
O SAY DOES THAT STAR-SPANGLED BANNER YET WAVE
O'ER THE LAND OF THE FREE AND THE HOME OF THE
BRAVE.

*(A **REAL SOPRANO** shows up.)*

THE SOPRANO. I'm a singer. May I join you?

ED. Please, please!

*(Since she sings so beautifully, **ED'S
PREVIOUS CUSTOMERS** reappear, gathering
around his stand to listen.*)*

THE SOPRANO.

MINE EYES HAVE SEEN THE GLORY OF THE COMING OF
THE LORD
HE IS TRAMPLING OUT THE VINTAGE WHERE THE GRAPES
OF WRATH ARE STORED;
HE HATH LOOSED THE FATEFUL LIGHTNING OF HIS
TERRIBLE SWIFT SWORD:
HIS TRUTH IS MARCHING ON
GLORY, GLORY HALLELUJAH!
GLORY, GLORY HALLELUJAH!
GLORY, GLORY HALLELUJAH!
HIS TRUTH IS MARCHING ON.

*(Soon the other customers join in, their
combined voices are glorious.)*

I HAVE SEEN HIM IN THE WATCH-FIRES OF A HUNDRED
CIRCLING CAMPS,

---

* A license to produce *Where Women Go* does not include a performance
license for any third-party or copyrighted music. Licensees should create
an original composition or use music in the public domain. For further
information, please see the Music and Third-Party Materials Use Note
on page iii.

THEY HAVE BUILDED HIM AN ALTAR IN THE EVENING
DEWS AND DAMPS;
I HAVE READ HIS RIGHTEOUS SENTENCE BY THE DIM AND
FLARING LAMPS:
HIS DAY IS MARCHING ON.
GLORY, GLORY HALLELUJAH!
GLORY, GLORY HALLELUJAH!
GLORY, GLORY HALLELUJAH!
HIS TRUTH IS MARCHING ON.

I HAVE READ A FIERY GOSPEL WRIT IN BURNISHED ROWS
OF STEEL:
AS YE DEAL WITH MY CONTEMNERS SO WITH YOU MY
GRACE SHALL DEAL;
LET THE HERO, BORN OF WOMAN, CRUSH THE SERPENT
WITH HIS HEEL,
SINCE GOD IS MARCHING ON.
GLORY, GLORY HALLELUJAH
GLORY, GLORY HALLELUJAH!
GLORY, GLORY HALLELUJAH
HIS TRUTH IS MARCHING ON.

HE HAS SOUNDED FORTH THE TRUMPET THAT SHALL
NEVER CALL RETREAT;
HE IS SIFTING OUT THE HEARTS OF MEN BEFORE HIS
JUDGMENT-SEAT;
OH, BE SWIFT, MY SOUL, TO ANSWER HIM! BE JUBILANT,
MY FEET!
OUR GOD IS MARCHING ON.
GLORY, GLORY HALLELUJAH!
GLORY, GLORY HALLELUJAH!
GLORY, GLORY HALLELUJAH!

(Singing the final verse.)

IN THE BEAUTY OF THE LILIES CHRIST WAS BORN ACROSS
THE SEA,
WITH A GLORY IN HIS BOSOM THAT TRANSFIGURES YOU
AND ME.

AS HE DIED TO MAKE MEN HOLY, LET US DIE TO MAKE
    MEN FREE,
WHILE GOD IS MARCHING ON.
GLORY, GLORY HALLELUJAH!
GLORY, GLORY HALLELUJAH!
GLORY, GLORY HALLELUJAH!
OUR GOD IS MARCHING ON.

    (Pause.)

KITTY BUCKLE. How about a little… "Messiah"?

    (The others in one voice.)

ALL. YES, YES! WE CAN PLAY AND SING THE FINAL
CHORUS TOGETHER!

ED. Don't laugh, but I actually sang in the choir of my
temple.

    (Everyone applauds.)

    *(***THE SILENT MAN WEARING A PARACHUTE***
starts running in circles putting his hands
to his ears, trying to tell everyone that he
actually heard* **ED** *singing.)*

PENNY. LOOK, LOOK, HE'S TRYING TO TELL US
THAT HE FLEW OVER THE TEMPLE AND HEARD
HIM SINGING OVER HIS STAND!!

    *(***ED*** *claps* **THE SILENT MAN WEARING A
PARACHUTE** *over the shoulder and the two
hug as the others coo "Awwww," moved.)*

    (Silence.)

KITTY BUCKLE. ON TO THE FINAL CHORUS OF THE
MESSIAH

    (The others cheer.)

SANDY WRENCH. *(Grabbing her cello.)* OK, ladies, time to get out our instruments again!

BLOSSOM PICK. *(Grabbing her recorder.)* Got it! Got it!

FREDDIE GONZALES. *(Grabbing her guitar.)* I'm ready when you are!

KITTY. *(To the others.)* Just wait! You won't believe how beautifully these women play together! But then again, women are *born* musicians!

> *(Once again, a recorded version of the final chorus of the "Hallelujah Chorus" plays as the women lean over their instruments.*)*

AND HE SHALL REIGN
AND HE SHALL REIGN
AND HE SHALL REIGN FOREVER AND EVER
KING OF KINGS (FOREVER AND EVER)
AND HE SHALL REIGN (HALLELUJAH! HALLELUJAH!)
AND HE SHALL REIGN FOREVER AND EVER
KING OF KINGS! AND LORD OF LORDS!
KING OF KINGS! AND LORD OF LORDS!
AND HE SHALL REIGN FOREVER AND EVER
FOREVER AND EVER
FOREVER AND EVER
HALLELUJAH! HALLELUJAH!
HALLELUJAH! HALLELUJAH!
HALLELUJAH!

> *(As* **THE SILENT MAN WEARING A PARACHUTE** *reappears in the distance, tossing out artificial flowers.)*

---

* A license to produce *Where Women Go* does not include a performance license for any third-party or copyrighted music. Licensees should create an original composition or use music in the public domain. For further information, please see the Music and Third-Party Materials Use Note on page iii.

(Then silence.)

THE OTHERS. *(With a gasp.)* We're in Heaven!

KITTY. What did I tell you?

THE OTHERS. *(Barely audible.)* Heaven...

> *(Ed's stand shimmers with heavenly light, making it seem to rise up into the air.)*

End of Play.